P9-EKD-794

RAINBOW
STREET
SHELTER

DISCOVERED!
A Beagle Called Bella

RAINBOW
STREET
SHELTER

DISCOVERED!
A Beagle Called Bella

by **Wendy Orr**

illustrations by **Patricia Castelao**

Henry Holt and Company ❖ New York

Henry Holt and Company, LLC
Publishers since 1866
175 Fifth Avenue
New York, NY 10010
mackids.com

Henry Holt® is a registered trademark of Henry Holt and Company, LLC.
Text copyright © 2013 by Wendy Orr
Illustrations copyright © 2013 by Patricia Castelao
All rights reserved.
Library of Congress Cataloging-in-Publication Data
Orr, Wendy.
Discovered! : a beagle called Bella / by Wendy Orr ;
illustrations by Patricia Castelao. — First edition.
pages   cm. — (Rainbow Street Shelter ; 6)
Summary: Mona at the Rainbow Street Shelter finds the perfect home—
and job—for an energetic beagle puppy who loves to sniff.
[1. Beagle (Dog breed)—Fiction. 2. Dogs—Fiction. 3. Animals—Infancy—
Fiction. 4. Working dogs—Fiction. 5. Animal shelters—Fiction.]
I. Castelao, Patricia, illustrator. II. Title.
PZ7.O746Di 2013   [Fic]—dc23   2012041301

ISBN 978-0-8050-9505-0 (HC)
1 3 5 7 9 10 8 6 4 2

ISBN 978-0-8050-9506-7 (PB)
1 3 5 7 9 10 8 6 4 2

ISBN 978-0-8050-9856-3 (ebook)

First Edition—2013 / Book designed by April Ward
Printed in the United States of America by
R. R. Donnelley & Sons Company, Harrisonburg, Virginia

For Melody, Harry, and Pippa,
and animals everywhere who need a
second chance to find their true home

—W. O.

Thanks to Wendy, Noa, and April
for sharing these marvelous books
with Claudia and me

—P. C.

RAINBOW
STREET
SHELTER

DISCOVERED!
A Beagle Called Bella

1

One spring night when all the humans were asleep, a floppy-eared brown and white beagle started having puppies. Her owner got up to sit beside her box, stroking her when she got tired and telling her what a good mother she'd be.

Five hours later, six puppies were nestled in the box beside her. The mother dog had licked them clean till they squirmed and mewled newborn puppy squeaks. She'd snuggled around them so they could wiggle up to her and drink her milk. Now they were resting after the adventure of being born, and the tired mother was going to sleep.

When the puppies grew up, they'd be brown and white with bits of black, like their mother, but right now they were black and white, except for their round

pink noses. Every one of them was as cute as a calendar picture. The owner would have loved to pick them up and cuddle them, but she knew the mother dog wouldn't want anyone else to touch them yet.

"Six adorable beagle puppies!" she said. "I wish I could keep you all. But you'll make whoever buys you very happy."

She hoped that selling them would make her some money too, but right now she didn't care about that. She just cared that they were all healthy and perfect.

The prettiest of all was the one who'd been born first. She was the first one to drink, and so she was the strongest. As the puppies grew over the next weeks, she would always knock the others out of the way if they were drinking where she wanted to. Her brothers and sisters rolled and tumbled and found another place to nurse; it was easier to let her do what she liked.

"You're a strong little girl!" the owner told her. "Whoever chooses you will have to make sure you don't boss them around."

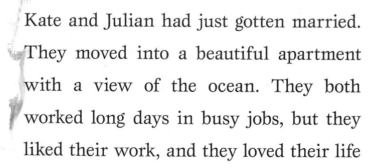

Kate and Julian had just gotten married. They moved into a beautiful apartment with a view of the ocean. They both worked long days in busy jobs, but they liked their work, and they loved their life together. On the weekends, they always had breakfast at their favorite coffee shop near the beach.

One chilly Saturday morning, it was so bright and beautiful that after breakfast they walked down to the beach and along the boardwalk. Lots of other people were out too, riding bikes, skating, or walking their dogs.

"You know what would be perfect?" said Kate.

"A dog," said Julian.

"We could go to the animal shelter on Rainbow Street," said Kate. "They must have lots of dogs."

"It'd be more fun to have a puppy

that we could train the way we want," said Julian.

They pulled out their phones and searched online as they walked.

CUTE BEAGLE PUPPIES!
Three males and three females.
All tricolor (black, brown, and white).
Ready to leave their mama in
3 weeks. Come and see them
now——be ready to fall in love!

The picture showed the prettiest puppies Kate and Julian had ever seen.

"Aww . . . ," said Kate.

Julian was already dialing. "Can we see them today?" he asked.

The puppies were even cuter in real life than they'd been in the picture. The black on their faces was fading to brown, and their pink noses had turned black. Their fur was soft as velvet.

Staggering around the kitchen floor on their short bowed legs, yipping with shrill puppy squeals, they tried to chase a soft blue ball with their mother. Sometimes they bumped into each other and stopped to wrestle, nuzzle, and lick as if they'd forgotten what they were doing.

"They're gorgeous!" Kate exclaimed.

"But she's the cutest," Julian said,

pointing to the bossy puppy who'd been born first.

They watched as she shouldered through the pack to get the blue ball. She hit it with her nose, jumping back in surprise when it rolled away. One of her brothers bumped into her, and they both tumbled over. The brother wandered away,

but the little girl puppy rolled back to her feet and started after the ball again.

"She's smart," said Julian.

"And beautiful," Kate murmured, as the owner picked up the puppy and put her into Kate's waiting arms. "You're the most beautiful little girl ever, aren't you?"

Smiling at each other over the puppy's head, Julian and Kate stroked the floppy velvet ears and the round bulgy belly. The baby beagle chewed on their fingers, wriggled against them, and licked their faces. Even her sour-milk puppy smell seemed sweet as roses.

The owner was smiling too. It made her happy to see people falling in love with a puppy.

"Her name is Bella," said Kate.

"Because she's so beautiful," Julian agreed. They had been studying Italian, and one of the first things they'd learned was that *bella* meant "beautiful."

"How are we going to wait three whole weeks before we take her home?" Kate asked. She could hardly bear to put the puppy down again, even though the mother dog was looking anxious and Bella was squirming.

"You can visit again next weekend," said the breeder. She knew this dog was going to a good home.

2

"Earth to Timothy!" the teacher called. "Can you hear me?"

Tim jumped. "Yes," he muttered.

"Would you like to share what you're thinking, since it's so much more important than anything I have to say?"

"Sorry," said Tim. "My dad's dog is

turning nine. Dad's picking me up after school to go to the retirement party."

A girl at the front of the room giggled.

"Sherlock's a sniffer dog," explained Tim. "After the party, he's going to come home to live with us."

His friend Josh clapped, as if Tim had made a speech. So did Hannah, the girl who loved pets so much that she volunteered at the Rainbow Street Shelter every week.

"That *is* exciting," the teacher agreed. "I think it would be very interesting to hear more about Sherlock's work some-time. But right now the rest of the class is getting ready for a spelling test, and I'd really like you to join in."

Tim blushed and picked up his pencil.

Sherlock was a beagle, and he'd been a sniffer dog most of his life. He worked with Tim's dad, Matt, at the airport, checking that people weren't bringing in any food or plants or animals that they weren't supposed to. It was very important work, because if bugs or diseases came in too, they could spread around the country.

Sherlock was good at his job. He'd walk along beside people's bags, sniffing as he went—and if he smelled the tiniest hint of plants, animals, or food, he sat down and didn't move till Matt told him to.

"Show me," Tim's dad would say, and

Sherlock would sniff at the pocket on the backpack or the corner of the suitcase where the smell was coming from.

He could smell so well that sometimes he sat down in front of a bag that someone had used for a picnic the week before, even though there was no food in it now. He'd smelled dog treats that people had forgotten were in their pockets and chocolate bars they'd forgotten in their purses.

But he'd also found lots of things that people knew they weren't allowed to bring and were trying to sneak in. He'd discovered papayas, grapes, lemons, mangoes, and nearly every other kind of fruit there was. Sometimes the fruit he found had fruit flies or other bugs, which was exactly why it wasn't allowed in. He'd sniffed out sausages and salamis hidden in socks, seeds tucked into shoes, wooden carvings full of woodworms, and even a giant python coiled in a suitcase.

He was still a very good detective, but he'd been a sniffer dog for many years. Now it was time for him to relax and enjoy being a stay-at-home dog.

Bella grew and got stronger day by day. Julian and Kate went to see her the next weekend, and the one after that, and they could hardly believe how much she changed each time.

The puppies still bumped into each

other, but hardly ever fell over when they did. They could run and were learning to climb and jump up on things, even though they didn't understand which things they were supposed to climb on and which they weren't.

What hadn't changed was that Bella was still the most beautiful, the strongest, and the smartest of them all. Tomorrow she would be eight weeks old, and Kate and Julian were going to bring her home.

That night after work they went to a huge pet store to buy her a soft, comfy dog basket. It was pink with a pattern of white bones, and as they walked around the store, they filled it up with toys. They chose a soft ball for Bella to roll, a teddy bear to comfort her when she was alone, and a squeaky rubber bone to chew.

They bought a water bowl, a food dish, a red collar and soft leash, special puppy kibble and canned dog food, puppy biscuits for treats, and a package of pee pads to put in the bathroom, for when they were at work and couldn't take her outside.

They woke up early on Saturday morning and were too excited about getting their new puppy to go out for breakfast. They had toast and coffee at home, tidied the kitchen, and they were ready to go.

Kate sighed with happiness. The sun was coming in the windows; the apartment was sparkly clean. Their beautiful puppy would soon be in her little pink bed in the corner, and everything would be even more perfect than it was now.

Another car was already at the beagle breeder's house when Kate and Julian got there.

"We're lucky we chose Bella first!" Kate whispered as they walked to the door. Luckily, the other family seemed very happy too. They had a son and a daughter, and they'd chosen a boy and a girl puppy. "The pups will be company for each other during the day," they told Kate and Julian, "and the kids will give them lots of exercise."

"Beagles do need lots of exercise!" the breeder agreed. "And you'll need to be firm with them. Start some training right away."

She kissed all three puppies on the top of their smooth little heads as she handed them to their new owners. "They've already had their first round of shots," she explained. "You'll have to take them to your own vets for the next ones in a couple of weeks. But love's the most important thing—lots of play and lots of love should give you long and happy lives together."

Kate and Julian smiled. They were ready to give their puppy all the love she needed.

Bella sat on Kate's lap on the way home. For the first ten minutes, she snuggled and squirmed, trying to climb up to lick Kate's face. For the middle ten minutes, she squirmed and tried to wiggle across to

Julian. For the last five minutes, she just squirmed as if she couldn't get comfortable. Finally, as they pulled into the parking lot, she threw up.

"I should have brought a towel," said Kate, wiping the mess off her new jeans with a tissue.

Julian took the puppy, snapped the little collar in place, and clipped on the leash. "We'd better keep her outside till she's finished." Bella had never worn a collar and leash before, but she didn't seem to mind. She didn't even mind that she'd just been sick. She waddled around the sidewalk, sniffing and squeaking.

"I wonder if she has to pee?" Julian asked.

"Let's wait a bit longer," said Kate.

Bella was too busy to pee; there were new smells to sniff and new things to see. She yipped shrilly at a boy on a skateboard, cowered at the hiss of a bus opening its doors, and bounded over to people walking past. Nearly everyone stopped to smile and say, "She's so cute!"

Julian and Kate felt very proud as they carried their new puppy up to their apartment.

An hour later, Kate had changed her jeans, Bella had peed on the floor, Julian had wiped it up and shown her the pee pad in the bathroom, Bella had had a drink of water, climbed into her water dish and tipped it over when she tried to get out, Kate had mopped it up and refilled the water dish with not quite so much water, Bella had chewed the ends off the laces of Julian's sneakers, and finally collapsed, asleep, in the middle of the floor.

Kate picked her up and laid her gently in the pink and white basket. The puppy didn't stir.

"She looks so sweet when she's asleep!" said Kate.

"She must be exhausted," said Julian. "The breeder said she'd need about twenty hours of sleep a day—she'll probably sleep for ages."

They tucked the teddy bear in beside the peaceful puppy, closed the door quietly behind them, and went out for lunch.

Bella slept for nearly an hour. Then a door slammed in the apartment upstairs. She woke up and found herself alone.

In all the eight weeks of her life, the beagle puppy had never been alone before. She'd never been more than a few feet from her mother and brothers and sisters. She was used to people being around as well, and the busy rush of family life.

With a quiet whimper, Bella started to cry. The whimper grew into a whine and finally a howl. It was the first time she'd howled. She liked the way it made her feel.

When she was bored with howling, she chewed gently on her teddy bear. The teddy bear fell over and made her jump, so she growled and wrestled it out of the basket. It was bigger than she was, but she dragged it around the floor until its ear came off. She left the teddy where it was, and after a while, dropped what was left of the chewed-up ear.

She began to explore the apartment. Julian and Kate had been so sure that she'd stay asleep that they hadn't closed the other doors. Kate's furry slippers were beside the bed. Bella crawled across them. They smelled of wool and Kate. She began to chew.

3

Matt and Tim had been worried that Sherlock would be bored, now that he wasn't working at the airport. But the very first evening that they brought him home, after the party with a dog food cake for Sherlock and a cake shaped like a dog bone for everyone else, the beagle had settled right in. He'd sniffed all over the house, checking every room and cupboard, and then settled down in his basket in the family room as if he'd lived there forever.

Now, every night after school, Tim took Sherlock for a walk. Sometimes when his dad got home, they all went for another long walk together, down to the beach or a fenced park where Sherlock could run free. But unless he had soccer practice or something else right after school, Tim always walked Sherlock first.

Two years ago, when Tim's mother had left home and gone to live halfway across the country, Tim had hated getting home from school. Sometimes he would go home with Josh and his dad would pick him up after work. Other times, Mrs. Gunther from next door would meet him at the school gate and take him back to her house till his dad got home.

Tim had known Mr. and Mrs. Gunther for as long as he could remember. They were like extra grandparents. Going home to Mrs. Gunther wasn't the same as going home to his mom, though.

Sherlock changed everything.

Tim walked home from school by himself now. He rang Mrs. Gunther's doorbell when he arrived, and she came over with him to prepare a snack and a drink.

And as soon as they opened the door, Sherlock was there waiting for them. He sniffed Tim up and down, as if he was finding out what the boy had been doing,

whom he'd seen, and what he'd eaten, and then he did the same to Mrs. Gunther.

No matter what Tim was eating, Sherlock was sure he needed some too. His eyes were so round and pleading, and he stared so hard, that it was very difficult to say no.

"You know what your dad says," Mrs. Gunther always reminded Tim when he tried to sneak half a cracker or a bite of cheese to the begging dog. "Beagles love to eat, but it's very easy for them to get fat."

But sometimes she gave in to the pleading eyes too, and cut a slice of apple or carrot especially for Sherlock. "At least that's healthy," she always said when Tim saw her doing it.

The only bad part about Sherlock living at home was that Matt didn't have a beagle to work with anymore. All dogs can smell, but not every dog can learn to be a sniffer dog and work in a busy airport. They need to have lots of energy so they can work all day, be very, very smart about what they're sniffing for, and stay calm and friendly around the people they meet.

Right now, there wasn't another dog who could do all those things. So until a new beagle was trained, Matt had to do more paperwork and other jobs he didn't like as much.

Tim knew his dad wouldn't be happy again till he had a dog to work with.

By the time she was a year old, Bella had chewed up two left sneakers, one pair of sandals, one high-heeled boot, one pair of jeans, and more socks and underwear than Julian or Kate could remember. She'd also chewed sunglasses, remote controls, and the spines off a whole shelf of books.

She'd been to the vet's emergency room when she couldn't stop vomiting after she'd eaten the lilies in a vase on the coffee table. She'd had another trip after she found the bowl of Halloween candy.

Bella had a chain leash now because she liked to chew on her leash whenever she had to stop on a walk. She could eat through a soft leash while they waited for a green light to cross the road. She'd eaten through a leather leash sitting at Julian's feet at an outdoor table at their favorite coffee shop. A boy skating past had helped them catch her before she ran into the road.

Julian and Kate had never had anyone in the back seat of their car, so they didn't know that Bella had eaten the back seat belts.

One day they forgot to close their bedroom door when they went to work. They came home and found the bedspread in the middle of the living room floor, white fluff scattered all over the apartment, and torn-up, empty pillow-cases in the bathroom. There was even more white stuffing in the bedroom, and a beagle-sized hole in the back corner of the mattress.

After that, they bought a crate for Bella to stay in when they weren't home, but their workdays were long, and she wasn't happy in the crate. The neighbors weren't happy either, because she howled most of the time she was in it.

Kate and Julian took turns jogging around the block with Bella before work, and again in the evenings. On the week-ends, if the weather was good, they took her for longer walks on the beach. They found a leash-free dog park where they could let her run around. The first few times, Bella ran away as soon as she was let loose. The park was fenced, but it sometimes took a long time to catch her. Then Kate and Julian learned to throw a ball for her the instant they unclipped her leash. She'd always come back with her ball, waiting for them to toss it again.

Bella loved playing ball. She liked jumping and catching, but what she liked best was chasing and finding a ball after a long, hard throw.

And even though she'd eaten lots of balls when she was home alone during the day, she never lost one when she was playing. It didn't matter how deep into the bushes the ball went or how far into the long grass, Bella could always find it.

Sometimes, if the ball landed in a mud puddle or a long way under a prickly bush, Julian or Kate gave up and threw her a new ball. Bella would rush to it, sniff it, and leave it there while she went on looking for the ball she wanted. They could never trick her.

So they were sure that she'd never run away if she had a ball to play with.

"Let's have an adventure, Bella!" said Kate when she got home early one afternoon. They drove to a leash-free beach. Kate sang, and Bella wagged her tail all the way.

Between the highway and the beach was a broad strip of land with scrubby bushes and trees. Hardly anyone else was there. They ran down to the beach to play ball.

But just as Kate unclipped Bella's leash, a rabbit ran out of the bushes. Bella bayed a deep hunting call and took off after it. Her nose was low to the ground, her tail

was waving, and she was running so fast that, in a moment, she was out of sight.

Kate ran desperately up and down the beach. "Bella," she shrieked. "BELLA!"

No beagle appeared.

She called Julian. He rushed from work and came to help her hunt for their runaway dog. They ran up and down the beach and through the bushes. Julian's voice was louder than Kate's, but it didn't make any difference: Bella didn't come back. Once Kate thought she heard her baying again, but they didn't ever see so much as the white tip of her tail.

Finally, when it was dark and they couldn't run anymore, they went home.

Timothy was waiting at the airport with his dad. Usually he loved going to the airport. It was like other kids going to their parents' offices. He felt proud when pilots greeted Matt and smiled at him. And he liked saying hello to the sniffer dogs who were working the same way Sherlock used to. If the dogs were wearing their jackets, they were on the job and he wasn't supposed to pet them, but it was okay if they weren't dressed yet.

But today Tim didn't feel like smiling or talking to anyone.

Today was the first time Tim would go

to see his mom all by himself. He was going to miss a week of school, but he had so many feelings swirling around inside that he didn't even know if he was happy or sad about that.

His dad was going to put him on the plane, and his mom and her new husband and baby would meet him when he landed. A flight attendant would look after him on the plane in between the airports, so he wouldn't really be alone.

But he felt alone.

A little part of him was excited about going on the plane himself, but another part was nervous. Somehow, even though his mom had moved so far away and he saw her only every few months, he'd always thought that she'd come back to him and his dad one day. When she got married again, he had to admit that wasn't true, and now that he had a baby brother, that trueness hurt all over again.

4

Bella had seen the rabbit for only an instant, but as soon as she turned toward it, she hit its trail. She had never smelled anything like this. The scent of it poured into her wet black nose and flooded her body, a thousand times stronger and better than the smell of tennis balls or chewy treats. She couldn't see or hear anything else—the scent said, "Follow me!" and she obeyed.

Sometimes the trail circled, and sometimes it zigzagged through the bushes. When she came to a place where a second rabbit had run across the first rabbit's path, she followed the second one, because her nose told her the trail was fresher.

If she'd been a person, Bella would have said that she was happier than she'd ever been in her life. But she was a dog, so she didn't stop to think about being happy or what she wanted to do. She just did it.

She ran till she couldn't run anymore. Her legs folded up, and she collapsed on the ground. She was panting hard, her long tongue was lolling out of her mouth, and her heart was racing. She was hungry and very thirsty. But she was too exhausted to move.

The world was dark and quiet. The little beagle stayed where she was and went to sleep.

In the middle of the night, the full moon came out from behind a cloud. It beamed white onto the sand, lit up the hollows and spaces in the bushes, and shone into Bella's eyes.

She stretched and stood up. For a moment, she felt lonely, but she was too thirsty to worry about anything else.

The sea glinted below her. Bella trotted down to it and lapped up great mouthfuls of salt water.

It tasted terrible. She shook her head in disgust and tried again. It still tasted terrible.

She trotted farther along the beach. The salt water in her belly made her vomit, but then she found a rotting fish in a pile of seaweed. Bella liked things that stank, so she ate the fish and then rolled in the smelly seaweed.

Back near the bushes, she found half an ice cream cone, still soggy with melted ice cream. Bella swallowed it hungrily—and then she smelled another rabbit.

She forgot that she was thirsty and tired. Her nose was telling her to run, and she ran. The rabbit led her in long, looping circles through the darkness. When it finally disappeared down a hole, Bella was farther than ever from where Kate had last seen her.

She collapsed under another bush and slept till dawn, her body twitching with exhaustion.

Kate and Julian hardly slept all night. They got to the beach just as the sun came up. It felt like the loneliest place they'd ever seen.

They jogged through the bushes where Bella had disappeared, calling and searching on different paths. Kate saw something brown behind a sand dune.

"BELLA!" Kate screamed. The brown lump didn't move. *She must be hurt*, Kate thought.

Julian raced back to her. Hearts thumping, they ran together around the dune to find a crumpled brown T-shirt under a bush.

Kate burst into tears. Julian nearly did too. If they had seen the tiniest sign of their beautiful dog, they would have stayed home from work to look for her. But they didn't know if she was alive or dead, somewhere near them or miles away.

"We should call the Rainbow Street Animal Shelter," said Julian. "Someone might have found her already."

But Mona, who answered the phone at Rainbow Street, said that no one had reported finding a dog. "Beagles can run a long way," she added. "We'll let you know if we hear anything at all. Don't give up!"

They called the local vets, and the city pound too, but no one had seen a lost beagle. Julian and Kate hugged each other tight and went to work. They knew it was going to be a long and miserable day.

The next time Bella woke up, she trotted the other way, from the beach toward the highway. She licked up pools of dew on the sidewalk and found some soggy chips in a torn bag. She was ready to go home.

The traffic got busier. Cars and trucks hurtled along the highway in the morning rush. Bella stood on the curb. Finally, she gave up waiting and raced into the road.

A car swerved and honked. Bella

streaked back to the side, her tail tucked tight with fear, and fled into the bushes. It didn't take long before she'd found the scent of another rabbit and was off.

But she wasn't the only one on the beach now. A man jogging down the path with a bull terrier heard her baying.

His own dog was old and obedient. He'd unclipped her leash because she could be trusted to trot along beside him and not run away. But her ears pricked now, and she veered off the path toward the sound of the hunting beagle.

The man called her back, but when Bella bayed again, closer, and he saw the white tip of a waving tail, he changed his mind.

"Okay," he told his dog, "let's go see what's happening. It doesn't look like that dog's got a person with it."

A second later, Bella raced across the path in front of them. She was filthy, stinky, and skinny after her day and night of running. She was very obviously lost.

"Come here, girl," the man called.

Bella kept on running.

He called again. She didn't seem to hear.

"SIT!" the man bellowed. Bella was so surprised that she sat. So did his dog.

"Stay," the man ordered, more quietly. "Good dog."

Offering her a chewy treat from his pocket, he clipped his own dog's leash onto Bella's collar.

With the beagle on the leash and his own bull terrier trotting obediently behind, they jogged back to his car. He loaded the two dogs in and drove to the Rainbow Street Animal Shelter.

5

Rainbow Street was short and narrow. At the end, surrounded by a tall wire fence, was a big garden with shady trees and green lawns. The building at its front was pale blue, with a bright rainbow arching over the cheery, cherry-red door.

The man who'd found Bella left his

own dog in the car and led the young beagle into the waiting room.

"Can I help you?" asked a gray parrot on a perch above the desk. He sounded exactly like an old man.

A woman with a name tag that said MONA and long dark hair wound up above a kind face came out from behind the desk. "I think I just talked to your owners!" she told the filthy beagle.

"I found her running in the bushes by the beach," the man explained. "She must have been hunting."

"She smells like she caught a dead fish," said Mona, crinkling her nose. "I'm afraid you're going to need a bath, little girl! But

I'm going to check your microchip first—
I'd hate to call the wrong owners."

The man waited while Mona ran a wand over Bella's shoulder. It beeped, and Mona cheered.

"What happens now?" the man asked.

"I'll call the pet registry and give them this bar code. They'll look it up to see who the owner is. I'm hoping it's the same couple who called earlier."

When Mona phoned Kate to tell her that Bella was at the Rainbow Street Animal Shelter, Kate was so happy and relieved that she could hardly believe it. "Is she really okay?" she kept asking.

"Tired and stinky, but completely healthy," said Mona.

Kate laughed and then groaned. "But we can't get there till after work," she said.

"No problem," said Mona. "She'll be fine here for a few hours."

She gave Bella a bath before she put her in a kennel, so she'd be clean for Julian and Kate to take home.

"Your people are going to be very happy to see you!" Mona said as she scrubbed, and the beagle shook muddy water drops all over her.

Julian and Kate decided to meet at the apartment so they could pick Bella up together. But when they got home, they found a note taped to their door.

Dear Mr. and Mrs. Fernandez,

I'm sorry to have to bring this up, but your dog's barking is becoming a problem. She wakes my baby up from her nap, and my husband, who works from home, cannot concentrate with all the noise.

Please be considerate of your neighbors and make sure this stops.

If the issue has not been addressed within two weeks, I will be talking to the apartment committee.

Yours truly,

Kelly Lawrence

(Your upstairs neighbor)

"Oh, no!" cried Kate. "What are we going to do?"

"I don't know how we can teach her to be quiet," said Julian. "Maybe we should move."

"We'll have neighbors wherever we are," said Kate.

They still had no idea what they were going to do when they arrived at the Rainbow Street Animal Shelter.

Bella barked excitedly when she saw her owners, and they hugged and petted her.

"We've been so worried!" said Kate as the beagle bounced around them. "But she's not even sorry."

"Dogs don't feel sorry because of something that happened yesterday," explained Mona. "She's just happy to see you now."

In fact, Bella was very excited because she'd smelled the guinea pigs in the small animal room and the rabbits in their enclosure. The shelter was a paradise of smells, and she was sniffing all of them.

"But we have a problem," said Kate, and told Mona about the letter.

"We've done everything we can think of to make her happy," said Julian.

"The problem is that beagles get bored easily," Mona said. "They find it very hard to be left alone in an apartment all day."

"But we love her. I can't bear to think of giving her away," said Kate.

"Even if we move, she'd still have to be alone while we're at work," Julian said. It was the hardest thing he'd ever had to say.

Mona was watching and listening carefully. She felt very sorry for them, but her job was to think about the animal first.

"Bella needs a home where she can be kept busy, with other dogs or people around. She needs lots of exercise and play and also some discipline—she has to know that she's not the boss and that she can't destroy your things."

"I don't think we can give her that," Kate said sadly. Julian shook his head in agreement.

"If you decide to leave her with us,"

Mona said, "I'll make very sure that the new owners understand what she needs before I let them take her home."

Kate and Julian looked at each other, their eyes filling with tears. They hugged their dog one last time and went home alone.

Bella's tail drooped as she watched them go. Mona sighed. She was sure it was the right thing to do, but that didn't stop her from feeling sad.

She led Bella out to the dog area in the backyard, picking up a tennis ball on the way. The beagle started dancing around her, leaping for the ball. Mona couldn't help smiling as she shut the gate.

The dog area had a dusty lawn in the middle, with two shady trees and a few bushes. The kennels were arranged in a big U around it. Each kennel had its own fenced run; some had one dog; some had

two—but Bella didn't seem to notice the other dogs. All she could concentrate on was the ball.

"You're going to be okay," Mona told her, the third time the young dog bounded back with the ball in her mouth. "You just need something to do."

6

Tim was hoping his mother would leave her new husband and baby at home when she met him at the airport. For just that little while, he wanted to pretend she was his mom and nobody else's, just the way she used to be. He wanted to pretend that she didn't have a husband called Chad.

But they were all there, waiting at the

gate for him. He saw his mom hand the baby to Chad, and then she was rushing toward him with her arms open wide and hugging him tight, tight, tight.

"Look how tall you are," she exclaimed when she finally let him go. "You've grown so much!"

She took his hand and led him across to where Chad was holding the baby. "Do you want to hold your brother?"

NO! Tim shouted inside.

He didn't say it. The baby was very little. His name was Bentley, though he seemed too small to have such a grown-up name. He was only ten days old. Tim didn't think he'd ever seen such a brand-new baby. He was afraid he'd drop it and his mom would be angry—but he knew it would hurt her feelings if he didn't try.

Bentley was wrapped up like a parcel in a soft blue blanket, with only his silvery-fuzzed head sticking out. Very carefully, Chad put the bundle into Tim's arms.

His mom hovered at his side. "Hold him like this," she said, placing Tim's hand behind the baby's head.

Tim looked down into his sleeping brother's round pink face. He smelled of baby powder and milk; his wet lips opened and shut, blowing bubbles like a goldfish. It was hard to believe that he was going to be a real person one day.

But it was hard to be angry with him

too, hard to be jealous of someone so small and helpless. Holding him made Tim feel a bit the way he did when Sherlock looked at him with his round brown eyes.

He was still very relieved when his mom lifted the bundle out of his arms again and tucked it expertly against her own shoulder.

Bella would have been happy for Kate and Julian to come and take her home, but she was happy at Rainbow Street too. From her run, she could see and hear ten other dogs and the birds in an aviary. She could smell all their different smells, the scent of the rabbits in their enclosure behind one wall and the cats behind another. She could watch Juan and Mona as they went in and out the back door, even if they weren't coming to the dog enclosure.

Of course, she liked it best when they came to see the dogs, and best of all when they spent time with her.

They spent a lot of time with her the first few days. First of all, she needed to be checked by a veterinarian to make sure she was healthy.

"Very healthy!" said the vet.

Now they needed to play with her and find out if she knew how to come, sit, and stay.

Bella did know how, but she did those things only when she felt like it, because Kate and Julian had been so worried about her being bored during the day that they just played with her when they got home. They thought she would be even more bored if she had to practice sitting or coming when she was called.

But Bella loved treats. She loved any food. So when Juan took her out to the dog lawn, Bella loved the games of getting a tiny piece of kibble every time she sat, or when Juan let her go at one side of the lawn and Mona called her at the other. Sometimes she got a piece of kibble when she came, and sometimes she got to play with the ball.

She learned very, very fast.

"You're a smart little girl," Mona told Bella.

"She'll need a family that can keep her really busy," said Juan.

"People with kids," Mona suggested.

But first they needed to find out for sure if she was gentle with people and other dogs. They watched how she acted when people came to the shelter to look at the dogs who were ready to be adopted and see if there was one who'd be right for them.

Bella always came to the front of her run, wagging her tail. Even a little boy who banged on her gate with his toy truck didn't frighten her. She thought everyone was her friend. And because she wasn't afraid, she never snapped or growled.

Every Saturday morning and Tuesdays and Thursdays after school, Hannah came to Rainbow Street. She'd started when she found a dog called Bear. Bear had gone back to the boy who owned him, but Hannah kept on volunteering, even when her parents let her adopt her own dog. She helped clean out the runs and cages, fed the animals, and petted them. But her favorite part was playing with the dogs.

When she saw Bella, she was glad her own little dog, Peanut, couldn't come to the shelter with her. He might have been jealous if he'd seen how much she liked Bella.

"This one loves playing ball," said Juan. "I bet you could train her to do anything for a ball game!"

Hannah threw the ball as hard as she could, up and down the yard. Bella caught it every time. Back and forth she ran, dropping the ball at Hannah's feet and leaping with impatience for the girl to throw it again.

Juan was sitting outside one of the other dog runs, patting a fluffy little black dog with a gray muzzle. She was too old to care about ball games, and Juan rubbed her head soothingly as he watched Hannah and Bella.

"Now that you've got a bit of that beagle bounce out of her," he said, "how about some training?"

Hannah took a handful of kibble for treats. "Sit, Bella," she said. She'd trained Peanut to sit, stay, and come when he was still a puppy, but she knew it would take longer for Bella, since she was already grown up.

Bella sat, and Hannah gave her a piece of kibble. "Good dog."

"We've been working on that one," Juan said proudly.

They practiced twice more. Bella's eyes were shining. She loved getting treats, but she loved being told she was a good dog even more.

Hannah got her to sit again. "Now, stay," she said, and stepped away. Bella was so excited that she leapt after her. Hannah started again. After six more tries, Bella could stay while Hannah walked ten steps from her.

"She's earned another game," said Juan. "We want to stop each training session before she's bored, so she always thinks it's fun."

"Peanut likes hide-and-seek," Hannah

said. "Mom makes him stay with her till I call him, but there isn't anywhere to hide here."

"I've got an idea," said Juan. He brought empty cardboard boxes out from the store-room, put a ball inside one of them, and scattered them around the yard.

"Find the ball," he said.

Bella raced straight to the box, nosed it over, and bounded back to Hannah with the ball in her mouth. "Clever girl!" said Hannah, and threw the ball across the yard as hard as she could.

"Good thinking," said Juan. "A ball game's much better than a food reward."

Bella wagged her tail yes, begging for

another turn. This was her new favorite game. She trembled with excitement each time Juan made her sit while Hannah hid the ball, then shot across the yard to the boxes. Often she got the ball the first time, but if Hannah had hidden it under a pile, she just nosed each box off until she got to the right one.

"This is one smart little dog," said Juan, and Bella wagged her tail as if she'd understood that too.

Hannah played tug-of-war with two Jack Russell puppies, jogged around the garden with a chubby Labrador, and then played ball again with Bella. She didn't stop till her shoulder was aching, but Bella was still bouncing.

"Can I talk about Bella at the assembly on Monday?" Hannah asked Mona. "She's so much fun!"

At the school assembly on the first Monday of every month, Hannah went up onstage and talked about one animal from the Rainbow Street Shelter who was ready to be adopted. It was always hard to choose, because all the animals needed homes.

"I thought you were going to choose a different animal this month," Mona said.

"I guess it would be good to talk about

the pets people don't notice so much," Hannah admitted.

"Bella will never have trouble being noticed," Mona agreed. "But I'm going to make very sure that whoever adopts her is looking for an energetic dog, not just a cute one."

Hannah walked slowly through the small animal room and the bunny and cat enclosures. Finally she decided to talk about a brown and white rabbit with long floppy ears.

The bunny was cuddly but shy. Someone looking for an animal to adopt might not notice him. Even when Mona took pictures of him for Hannah to show at the assembly, it was hard to get one where he wasn't trying to hide. But the longer Hannah stroked his soft fur, the more she wanted him to find the person he belonged with. Bella might be bouncier and fun to play with, but this bunny deserved a good home too.

7

Tim missed Sherlock the whole week he was visiting his mom. He missed his dad too. That was worse because it was all mixed up: it was homesick hurting and being guilty for having a good time and feeling sorry for his dad, all rolled into one. Matt tried to sound happy when he talked to Tim on the phone, but he wasn't a good actor, and Tim hated having to pretend back. It made him feel like his head was going to explode.

Missing Sherlock was different. It was a simple kind of missing. He just wished he could put his arms around the dog's warm, solid body.

His mother didn't like dogs. That's why they hadn't had one when she'd lived with them. Dogs weren't hygienic, according to his mom. She talked a lot about cleanliness and hygiene, and even without a dog in sight, she kept scrubbing everything in case the baby got sick.

Tim thought she was probably right

about dogs. Sherlock did all the unhygienic things she complained about: he licked his own bottom, sniffed telephone poles where other dogs had peed, and ate disgusting bits of squashed food on the sidewalk.

His mom didn't seem to know that dogs could also make the most revolting smells in the world, so Tim didn't tell her that Sherlock was a champion at them. He didn't tell her that he and his dad just groaned, "Gross, Sherlock!" and opened the windows when it happened.

But he told her all the good things about Sherlock. Even if she didn't like dogs, she wanted to hear all about Tim's life, and Sherlock was part of it. They talked about school and soccer and his friends too. She asked about Josh and said to say hello to Mrs. Gunther.

On Saturday afternoon, Chad looked after Bentley while Tim and his mom went to the aquarium. They rode in a glass-bottomed boat and were given fish-feed pellets to throw in. Looking through the glass beneath their feet made it feel as if they were floating in the water with the hungry, brightly colored fish.

At the next tank, the guide chose Tim to ring a bell. Four giant stingrays swam to the surface to be fed. Tim and his mom learned how to hold the fish, sticking out through their fists, so that the stingrays could take them before flapping away on their great white wings. One of them spurted water back at them. Tim laughed, and his mom didn't even complain that it wasn't hygienic.

But that evening, and Sunday morning before they went to the airport, she kept talking about the baby, as if she wanted to make sure that Tim would remember all about him when he was home with his dad.

"Bentley's lucky to have a big brother like you," she kept saying. She showed him pictures of when he was a baby. "See how much you look alike? You'll be great buddies when he's older."

Tim couldn't really tell if his baby pictures looked like his brother or not. They were both round pink faces sticking out of blue-wrapped bundles. He knew it was true that Bentley was going to grow into a toddler, learn to walk and talk, and get old enough to go to school and be a normal kid, but it was still hard to believe.

And right now Bentley was a baby, who threw up every time he was fed and needed his diapers changed. He wasn't any more hygienic than Sherlock—and a lot less fun.

But it was just as hard saying good-bye to his mom as it had been saying good-bye to his dad the week before. Tim even felt

a little bit sad about saying good-bye to
Bentley.

Matt and Sherlock met Tim at the airport,
though Sherlock had to stay in the car in
the parking lot. When Tim got there, the
dog sniffed him all over, and then
sniffed his backpack all over too, as
if to prove he could still do it.

But then he licked Tim's face, and sniffer dogs never do that when they're working. He was very, very happy to have his boy home.

"Almost as happy as I am!" Matt laughed, and hugged Tim again.

Tim hadn't seen his dad this happy for a long time. "Are you getting another dog to work with?" he asked.

"Still waiting," said his dad. "There just aren't enough dogs to go around right now."

"It's too bad Sherlock couldn't still go to work with you sometimes."

His dad rubbed the beagle's floppy ears. "This guy's earned his retirement. And it's good having him at home, isn't it?"

Tim nodded. He would have hated for Sherlock not to be there when he got home from school in the afternoon, or not to wake him up with his wet beagle nose in the morning. At his mom's house, he'd usually woken up because Bentley was crying, and if the baby wasn't crying, his mom tried to sleep in, so Tim had to stay in his room and be quiet. But Sherlock's funny face and wagging tail made him laugh every morning—and there was no point staying in bed any longer than he wanted to, because he knew that the dog would have already woken up his dad, at seven o'clock on the dot.

In her run at the Rainbow Street Animal Shelter, Bella was watching Juan. He was feeding all the dogs in turn, but there were still three more ahead of her. She was already drooling by the time he opened her gate.

"You're not hungry, are you, Bella?" Juan teased, hiding the scoop behind his back.

Bella licked her lips, nosing around his legs.

"Can't fool you," he laughed. "If I can't hide a ball from you, I should have known you'd sniff out food anywhere!"

8

At the Monday morning assembly, Hannah stood up and talked about the brown and white lop-eared rabbit who needed a home. "If you're thinking about getting a pet, you should go to the Rainbow Street Animal Shelter and see him. He looks cute in this picture, but if you feel how soft he is and

see him twitching his nose, you'll love him even more."

Maybe Dad could have a sniffer rabbit, Tim thought, smiling at the thought of a bunny in a jacket checking the suitcases at the airport. *Except it would probably only sniff out carrots.*

But on Friday afternoon, when he looked out the window and saw Mona from Rainbow Street walking through the playground with her dog, Nelly, Tim suddenly remembered his sniffer bunny joke.

"I can't believe I never thought of Rainbow Street Shelter before!" He could hardly wait till the end of school; he wanted to run straight out of class to follow Mona.

On Friday afternoons, Mona brought Nelly to hear the little kids read. They all loved reading to the round brown dog, and even kids who weren't good readers, or who got nervous reading out loud to the teacher and other grown-ups, were happy to read to Nelly.

Tim could read easily now, but he knew why the little kids liked reading to Nelly. It was like telling Sherlock something— the dog never seemed to think he was stupid, even when he'd done something that everyone else in the world would have said was dumb.

So if Sherlock could talk, he'd say Tim's idea was worth a try.

Tim was the first out of the class when the bell rang.

He raced around to the door where the little kids came out. Mona was standing just inside the door, and the kids were stopping to pat Nelly good-bye as they passed. Tim waited impatiently.

Finally, when all the kids had straggled out, Tim stepped in. His mouth was dry.

Mona smiled at him. It was a nice smile. It made him feel safe, like he could ask her the craziest question, and she wouldn't laugh.

"Do you ever get any beagles at the shelter?" he asked.

At nine o'clock on Saturday morning, Tim, his dad, and Sherlock walked up the path to the cheery, cherry-red front door under the bright painted rainbow. They laughed at the parrot who thought he was the receptionist and said hello to Nelly. Then Mona led them through to the dog enclosure.

Sherlock trotted calmly beside Matt. There were eight other dogs there, all barking hello, but the beautiful young beagle was the only one they noticed. They went straight to her run.

Bella crept toward Sherlock with her nose on her front paws, her bottom in the air, and her tail waving wildly.

"She's asking him to play," Mona said, "and telling him that she knows he's the boss."

"Here, Bella!" said Tim's dad.

The beagle looked up and crossed to his side.

Sherlock wagged his tail. Matt smiled. Tim felt like happiness was bursting out all over his body.

"What happens if she can't be trained to be a sniffer dog?" asked Mona. "I don't want the poor girl to have to come back here again."

"We'd be happy to have two dogs, wouldn't we, Tim?" said his dad. "She'd be easier to control with an older dog at home to keep her company during the day. And our yard's already beagle-proof."

So they adopted Bella, and two weeks later, she went on to her training course to become a sniffer dog.

If Tim hadn't known how badly his dad

wanted a working dog again, he'd have hoped that Bella would fail her training so she could live with them. But he did know, so he was hoping nearly as much as his dad for her to pass.

Tim's dad took Tim and Sherlock over to Rainbow Street one night after work, to tell Mona how Bella was doing.

"She's a star!" he said.

Tim rubbed Sherlock's ears; he didn't want the old dog to get jealous.

"Her first owners will be pleased to hear that too," said Mona. "I can tell them tomorrow when they come to pick up their new friend." Because even though Julian and Kate knew that they couldn't handle a lively dog like Bella, their apartment seemed empty with her gone. So they'd had a long talk with Mona about what pet would be right for them, and now they were building a hutch for the brown and white lop-eared rabbit.

"Maybe you could let me know how the rest of Bella's training goes," Mona added.

"I'd like that," said Matt.

Training was the most fun Bella had ever had in her whole life. The only thing she hated was being bored, and now she was busy, busy, busy all the time. Some of the dogs got sick of the games and wouldn't go on, some got stressed, some didn't like being around so many people. All those dogs were sent home, but Bella passed every test.

Now she'd live with the other sniffer beagles at night and work with Matt during the day, just like Sherlock used to.

On her very first day working at the airport, Bella wore her brand-new jacket and walked along the line of people getting their suitcases off the luggage carousel, sniffing as she went. She didn't even need to stop to know that there weren't

any foods, plants, or animals in the bags. "Nothing interesting," her nose told her each time. Or "Sweaty clothes, tennis ball . . . but no food."

Suddenly she smelled something interesting in a bag off to the side. Wagging her tail happily, Bella walked straight over to the woman holding the bag and sat down in front of her. People stared. The woman blushed.

"Would you mind opening your bag?" said Matt. He put on his rubber gloves and pulled an apple core out of the side pocket.

"Good girl," he said to Bella, giving her a chewy treat. "Clever dog!"

Bella gobbled the treat.

The woman blushed even redder. "I was eating an apple when I got off the plane," she explained, "and I couldn't see a trash can, so I just dropped the core into my bag. I didn't think it would matter."

"It matters," said Tim's dad. "But mistakes happen." He was smiling; he knew the woman hadn't meant to do anything wrong, and he was very pleased with Bella.

Bella was happy too. She loved chewy treats, and she loved Matt patting and praising her. Most of all, she loved the game of sniffing.

She wagged her tail again, and when Matt nodded, she walked on past the next line of people and bags, reading all the scents that her clever beagle nose sniffed in.

The next Saturday, Tim and his dad, Sherlock, Nelly, and Mona met at a beach-side café to celebrate Bella's success.

"It's all thanks to Tim," said his dad. "If he hadn't thought of asking you about beagles, I still wouldn't have a dog to work with."

"And Bella would still be bored without a job to do," said Mona.

Tim was glad his idea had worked out so well. Even better, his dad was smiling again. But the sun was shining, the beach stretched long and white in front of them, and the adults had just ordered more coffee. "Can I take Sherlock for a walk?" hc asked.

"Nelly would love to go too," said Mona, when Matt had nodded yes.

The dogs jumped up from under the table, watching Tim expectantly. He took their leashes and jogged down the beach, the solid old beagle on one side and the little round dog on the other.

Come to Rainbow Street Shelter
and meet your new best friend!

Some of the pets are lost.
Some of them have never had a home.
But all of them need someone to love.